This
MOUSE WORKS
Classics Collection Storybook

belongs to

JVSTIN

DISNEY ✧ PIXAR

a bug's life

C L A S S I C S T O R Y B O O K

MOUSE ▦ WORKS™

Find us at **www.disneybooks.com** *for more Mouse Works fun!*

© 1998 Disney Enterprises, Inc./Pixar Animation Studios
Adapted by T. Jeanette Steiner.
Illustrated by Scott Tilley, John Skewes, Kory Heinzen, Sue DiCicco, and Andrew Phillipson.
Printed in the United States of America.
ISBN: 1-57082-979-9
1 3 5 7 9 10 8 6 4 2

Down under our feet, in among the clover and grass, there's another world. It's a tiny world, but it has mighty tales to tell...

"Do we have enough food for the offering?" Princess Atta asked nervously.

2

3

A young ant named Flik rushed up. "Look, Princess!" he cried. "An automatic harvester!" Atta glanced at the Queen. Now what? "Just pick grain like everyone else, Flik," she said. "We don't have time for one of your inventions."

But Atta's little sister, Dot, liked Flik. She thought he was special.

Dot always went to Flik with her problems. "My mom always says I'm too little to do things," she complained.

"You won't always be little," Flik pointed out. He showed her a rock. "Pretend this is a seed. Give it time, and it will be a tree. Just give yourself some time."

Dot knew the "seed" was a rock. "You're weird," she replied. "But I like you."

Suddenly the alarm sounded. The frightened
ants scattered.
The Queen took charge and urged everyone
into the anthill.
"Quickly, dear," she told Dot.

"Hey! Wait for me!" Flik called. But his wonderful harvester knocked the legs out from under the offering stone. All the grain the ants had collected rolled off the cliff and disappeared.

As the ants trembled in their anthill, the grasshopper
gang burst through the ceiling. "Where's my food?"
Hopper demanded, grabbing Dot. "If you don't keep
your end of the bargain, someone could get hurt."

Flik didn't think twice. "Leave her alone!"
he demanded.

One sharp look from Hopper silenced Flik. Then
Hopper dropped Dot. "I want double the order of
grain when the last leaf falls!" he snarled.

Once Hopper left, Atta and the Council were ready to banish Flik forever.

But Flik had an idea. "We could get bigger bugs to fight the grasshoppers!" he shouted. "I'll go to The City and find them!"

Surprisingly, Atta and the Council accepted his offer—but only to get rid of him.

15

Dot and a couple of ant boys followed Flik to the edge of Ant Island. "My dad says you're gonna die," one of the boys sneered.

"He's not gonna die," Dot stated. "He's gonna get the bestest, roughest bugs ever." She waved as Flik sailed away on a dandelion puff.

Far from Ant Island, near The City, P.T. Flea had to do something fast! The audience wasn't laughing at his circus.

18

"Flaming Death!" the desperate circus
manager announced.

The act went all wrong. The circus bugs
scrambled around trying to put out the fire,
but P.T. ended up barbecued.

The audience loved it. P.T. fired all his
performers anyway.

A little later, Flik arrived in The City. What a place! Surely here he would find bugs rough enough to stand up to Hopper.

23

The circus bugs were sitting in a bug bar, wondering what to do next. All of them needed new jobs—Rosie the spider and her beetle "steed" Dim, Slim the walking stick and Heimlich the caterpillar, Tuck and Roll the pill bug acrobats, Francis the ladybug, Manny the mantis magician and his moth assistant, Gypsy.

Then some rowdy flies picked a fight with Francis.

When Flik walked in on the fight, the small troupe of circus bugs looked like the winners.

Flik started clapping. "I've been scouting for bugs with your talent!" he told them. "Could you help my ant colony?"

The circus bugs thought he was a talent scout. "Explain on the way there," Slim suggested.

"This is too good to be true!" Flik said to himself.

The next morning, Flik and the circus bugs approached Ant Island.

Dot was the first to spot them. "Flik! I knew you could do it!" she shouted.

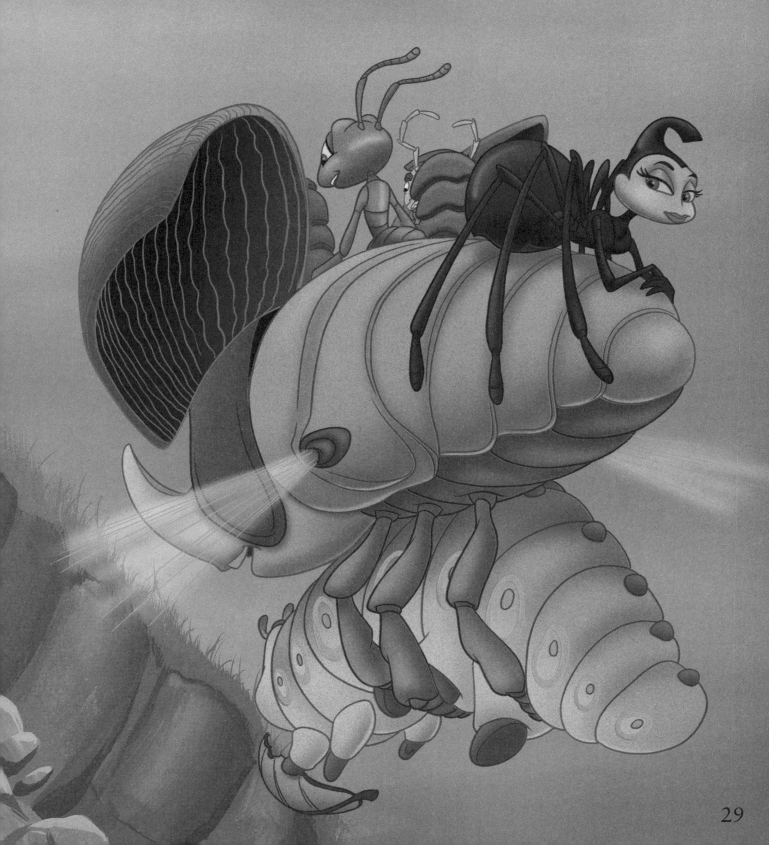

But the other ants were afraid of the big, rough bugs.

"We're losing the job," Slim worried.

Francis made an announcement. "When your grasshopper friends get here, we're gonna knock 'em dead!" he bragged.

"So, Princess Atta, what do you think?" Flik asked her.

"We're ants; we don't fight grasshoppers," she answered.

"No, but they will," he told her, pointing to the circus bugs.

The colony gave the circus bugs a welcome banquet. The ant children performed a play about the coming battle with Hopper.

"You mean that's us fighting?" Rosie whispered.

"Don't watch!" Slim warned Heimlich.

Rosie tried to get Flik's attention, but he was busy making a speech.

"Flik!" Rosie hissed. "We're circus performers!"

Flik followed the circus bugs away from the banquet. "Circus bugs?" he yelled. "You said you were gonna knock the grasshoppers dead!"

"You said you were a talent scout!" Manny accused. The circus bugs took off, hoping to find a new gig.

Flik grabbed Slim. "Don't go!" he begged. "They'll call me a loser!"

The circus bugs were trying to pull Flik away from Slim when Flik suddenly turned and sprinted away, yelling, "Run!"

A bird rose up from the grass behind Flik!
Screaming, all the bugs scrambled to find
a place to hide.

The screams brought the ants to the cliffs. Atta spotted the circus bugs running from the bird. Then she saw her little sister. Dot had followed Flik, and now she was directly in the bird's path!

Francis couldn't let Dot be hurt. He caught her, but they both tumbled into a crack in the riverbed.

The bird knocked stones into the crack. One stone broke Francis's leg; another knocked him out. Then the bird began pecking at the crack.

Flik quickly thought up a plan. Slim held up the tasty-looking Heimlich to distract the bird while the other bugs flew to the rescue.

"How brave!" one of the council members murmured.

As the others placed Francis in Rosie's net, Flik comforted Dot. His plan was working as smoothly as spider silk.

Dim was lifting the rescue party out of the crack when the bird saw them!

Good old Dim came through. He zipped into a thorny bush, where the bird couldn't follow.

Then Flik and the circus bugs heard a strange sound. "What's that?" Heimlich wondered.

It was applause. The whole ant colony was cheering wildly for the brave bugs who had saved their precious little princess Dot.

Later, Atta took Flik aside. "When you brought them here, I thought you'd hired a bunch of clowns," she said. "But they were so brave! Not every bug would face a bird. Even Hopper's afraid of birds." Flik felt an idea coming on.

Flik's plan was simple: build a bird to
scare off Hopper and his gang. He got
Manny to present the plan to the Council.
Atta and the Council loved it.

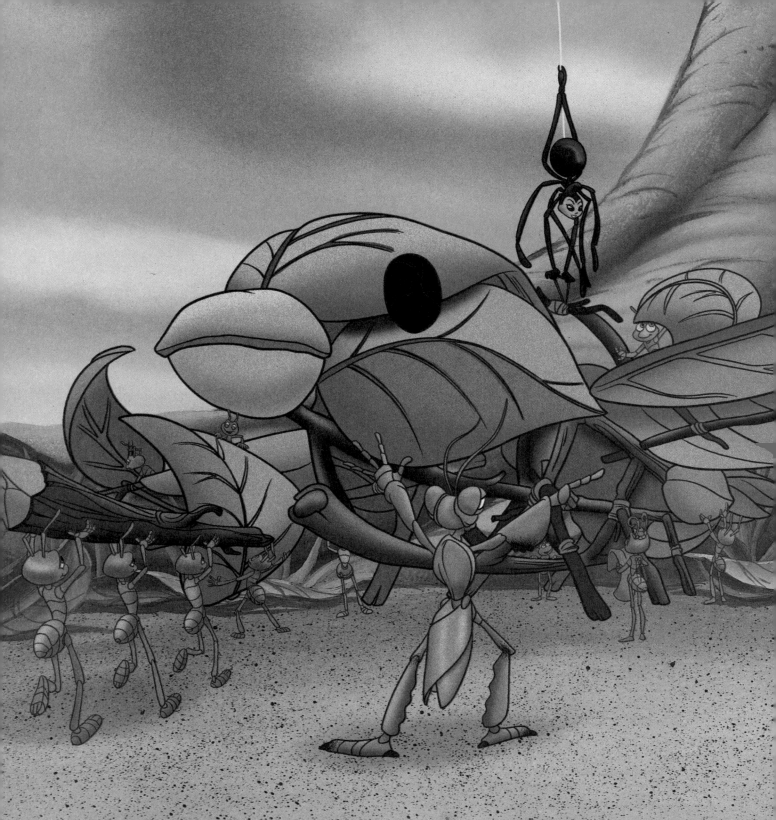

The ants and circus bugs worked together. Little
by little, the bird was shaped by leaves and twigs,
spider's web and snail shell. Everyone felt upbeat.
The grasshoppers' next visit would be very different!

Atta was proud to be part of a plan that would defeat the grasshoppers. It was all thanks to the warrior bugs—and to Flik, who had found them.

Finally, ever so carefully, the ants and warrior bugs raised the bird into the tree, where it would await Hopper's arrival.

A cheer went up. They were ready to rumble!

Meanwhile, the grasshopper gang was hanging out south of the border. A couple of Hopper's thugs didn't want to return to Ant Island. They convinced Hopper's brother, Molt, to present their case to their leader.

Hopper was furious. He buried the
mutineers under a pile of grain. Then he
snarled, "Those ants outnumber us. We
can't let them figure that out. We gotta
remind them who's boss! Now, let's ride!"
The grasshoppers took off for Ant Island.

Later that evening, Flik offered the circus bugs a chance to leave before the grasshoppers showed up.

"Dim don't want to go," the rhino beetle announced.

The others quickly agreed. The circus bug warriors were staying.

Suddenly an ant scout spotted someone approaching. But it wasn't the grasshoppers, it was P.T. Flea. He was looking for his circus bugs.

Flik tried to keep the secret, but the ants realized that their brave "warriors" were...circus bugs?

Hopper would be there soon, and they had no food! The
Queen told the circus bugs to go away.
Atta told Flik to leave, too.
Dot wanted to follow them, but her mother held her back,

All too soon, the ants heard the grasshoppers approaching.
"Mother!" Atta gasped desperately. "What can we do?"
Both of them knew that Hopper would be furious.

Hopper *was* furious. "No ant sleeps until we get every scrap of food!" he snarled.

While Dot was hiding from the grasshoppers, she learned Hopper's real plan. "Work 'em till they're dead," one of his thugs sniggered. "Then we squish the Queen."

Dot had to get help. Away she went, looking for Flik and the circus bugs.

She found them feeling sorry for themselves. "You gotta help us!" she gasped. "Hopper's gonna squish my mom!"

The circus bugs wanted to help. They tried to convince Flik that his bird idea would work, but he didn't agree.

Dot knew what Flik needed. "Pretend it's a seed," she said, showing him a stone.

Flik smiled. "All right!" he cried. "We'll do it!"

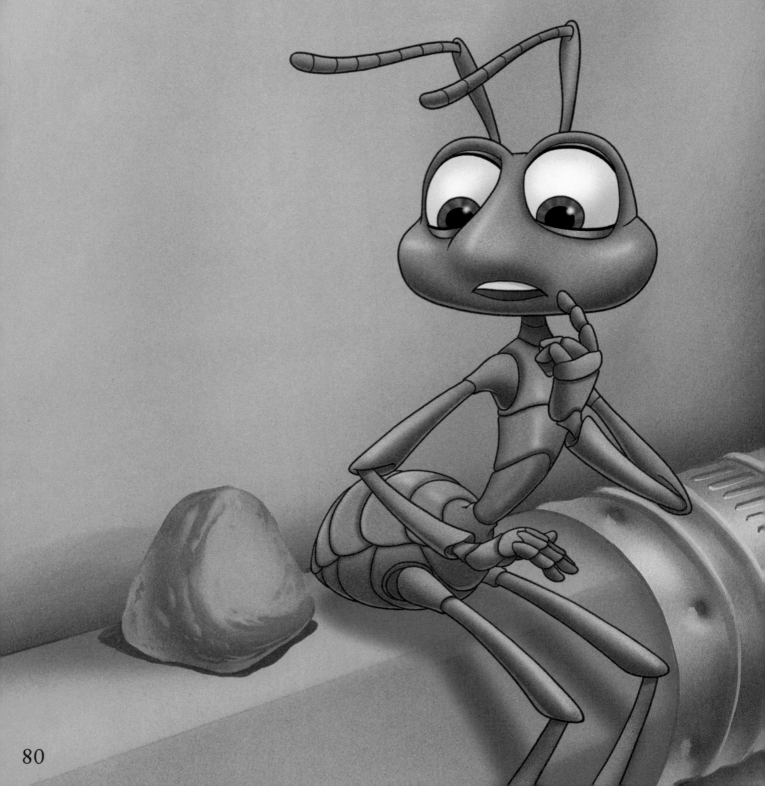

Flik and Dot slipped into the Blueberry hideout. "Ready to make some grasshoppers cry?" Flik asked the ant children.

"It's payback time, Blueberry-style!" Dot promised.

At a signal from Gypsy, the bird sprang from the knothole. From inside the cockpit, the screams of Flik and the Blueberries were amplified into the terrifying screech of a real bird!

The grasshoppers dived for cover.

The circus bugs and the ants reinforced the grasshoppers' terror with berry juice "blood." They had Hopper fooled until P.T. Flea, trying to save everyone, set the bird on fire. When Flik and the Blueberries bailed, Hopper knew he'd been tricked.

Hopper turned on Flik. "You're losers!" he raged.
Flik stood up to him. "You're wrong!" he
shouted back.

Inspired by Flik, the ants and circus bugs
charged. Soon the grasshoppers were in
retreat, and Hopper stood alone.

Suddenly huge drops of rain began crashing down.
As everyone ran for cover, Hopper took Flik hostage. The
circus bugs chased Hopper, but they couldn't catch him.
At the last minute, Atta snatched Flik away.
Hopper was furious!

Flik and Atta flew to the other side of the river.
Then Flik lured Hopper toward a nest.
The bird rose up with a screech. Hopper thought
this was another of Flik's tricks, but he was wrong!
And that was the end of Hopper.

Soon it was spring. With the Queen retired, Princess Atta was now Queen Atta. Her sister Dot now wore the princess crown, and her special friend Flik held an honored place as the colony's official inventor.

As the circus bugs left on tour, they all felt happy. Never again would the ant colony have to worry about going hungry. Their courage had finally freed them from the greedy grasshopper gang.